This Walker book belongs to:

For all my big and little friends at
Little Friends, especially Debbie, Rosemary,
Barb, Kari, Brie, Becca, Eric and Stefan
C. L. S.

For my family
V. C.

First published 2000 by Walker Books Ltd
87 Vauxhall Walk, London SE11 5HJ

This edition published 2009

2 4 6 8 10 9 7 5 3

This book has been typeset in Maiandra GD

Printed in China

British Library Cataloguing in Publication Data:
a catalogue record for this book is available from the British Library

ISBN 978-1-4063-2489-1

www.walker.co.uk

Down in the Woods at Sleepytime

Carole Lexa Schaefer illustrated by Vanessa Cabban

WALKER BOOKS
AND SUBSIDIARIES
LONDON • BOSTON • SYDNEY • AUCKLAND

Deep down in the woods,
Mama Bear says, "It's sleepytime."

"No, uh-uh," grumble her cubs.
"We still want to play."

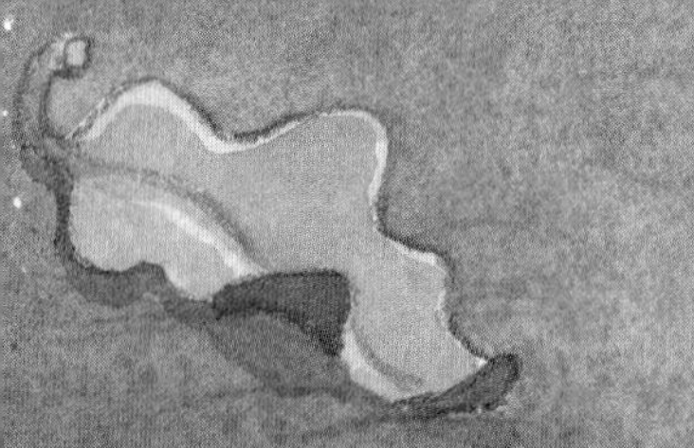

And they clown around

in the scruffy brush.

Deep down in the woods,
Mama Hedgehog says, “It’s sleepytime.”

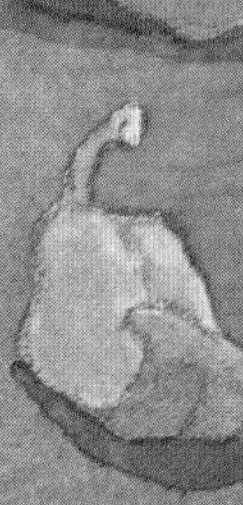

“No, uh-uh,” squeal her prickly babies.
“We’re still hungry.”

And they snuffle for snacks

in the mossy grass.

And hip-hop, they hide

under fat green leaves.

Deep down in the woods,
Mama Toad says, “It’s sleepytime.”

“No, hmm-mmm,” hum her toadlets.
“We’re still making up songs.”

Wise Grandma Owl
blinks her big eyes.
She looks around...

"*Whoo-hoo,*" hoots wise Grandma Owl.

"*Sweet*

dreams."

Also by Carole Lexa Schaefer

ISBN 978-0-7636-2006-6

Other books illustrated by Vanessa Cabban

ISBN 978-0-7445-8950-4

ISBN 978-1-84428-521-1

ISBN 978-1-4063-0596-8

ISBN 978-1-4063-1957-6

Available from all good bookstores

WALKER BOOKS